The giraffe has the longest tail of any land mammal.

Giraffes need high blood pressure and a rapid heartbeat to pump blood all the way up to their heads. They have special blood vessels that keep the blood from rushing to or from their head when they raise or lower it. Otherwise, they would faint every time they tried to take a drink.

Giraffes have hard hooves and their kick can be deadly. How rude!

While at Case Western Reserve University studying for my degree
in civil engineering, I met many inspiring women doing the same.
This book is dedicated to them and to
all women (and girls!) in science and engineering. —J. A.

To Alice and Bo—Y. I.

MARGARET K. McELDERRY BOOKS
An imprint of Simon & Schuster Children's Publishing Division
1230 Avenue of the Americas, New York, New York 10020
Text copyright © 2018 by Jim Averbeck
Illustrations copyright © 2018 by Yasmeen Ismail
All rights reserved, including the right of reproduction in whole or in part in any form.
MARGARET K. McELDERRY BOOKS is a trademark of Simon & Schuster, Inc.
For information about special discounts for bulk purchases, please contact Simon &
Schuster Special Sales at 1-866-506-1949 or business@simonandschuster.com.
The Simon & Schuster Speakers Bureau can bring authors to your live event. For more
information or to book an event, contact the Simon & Schuster Speakers Bureau at
1-866-248-3049 or visit our website at www.simonspeakers.com.
Book design by Ann Bobco
The text for this book was set in Big Caslon.
The illustrations for this book were rendered in watercolor and colored pencil.
Manufactured in China
0318 SCP
First Edition
2 4 6 8 10 9 7 5 3 1
Library of Congress Cataloging-in-Publication Data
Names: Averbeck, Jim, author. | Ismail, Yasmeen, illustrator.
Title: Two problems for Sophia / Jim Averbeck ; illustrated by Yasmeen Ismail.
Description: New York : Margaret K. McElderry Books, 2018.
Summary: "Sophia is happy to have Noodle, her One True Desire, yet her new pet
comes with two giraffe-size problems"—Provided by publisher.
Identifiers: LCCN 2016004072 | ISBN 978-1-4814-7788-8 (hardcover : alk. paper) |
ISBN 978-1-4814-7789-5 (eBook)
Subjects: CYAC: Giraffe—Fiction. | Pets—Fiction. | Family life—Fiction.
Classification: LCC PZ7.A933816 Tw 2018 | DDC [E]—dc23
LC record available at https://lccn.loc.gov/2016004072

Two Problems for Sophia

by
jim averbeck
and
yasmeen ismail

Margaret K. McElderry Books
New York London Toronto Sydney New Delhi

Sophia felt happysad—
happy to have Noodle,
  her One True Desire,
yet sad that her new pet came
  with giraffe-size problems.

The first was his tongue.

ewwwww!

When Noodle kissed you, his eyelashes danced a little fluzzle,
then his nose swooped in for a nuzzle, and then . . .

SLUUUURP

UGH!

He was especially fond of Grand-mamá.

The feeling was not mutual.
"I can't bear a sloppy kiss,"
said Grand-mamá.
"And besides, he snores."

Snoring was the second problem.

ZZZZRRRRRR-WAHWWOOOOOOOOOMP

ZZZZRRRRRRR-WAHWWOOOOOOOOOMP

When Noodle slept,
no one else could.

Mother rendered her verdict at breakfast.

"Noodle is guilty of robbing this family,"
she said, "of sleep! I hereby order you to
find a perdurable solution to his problems."

"Perdurable?" asked Sophia.
"What's that mean?"

"Permanent," said Mother. "Forever."

Noodle tried to make up with Grand-mamá.
His eyelashes fluzzled, his nose nuzzled, and then . . .

SLUUUURP

"Like sending him back,"
muttered Grand-mamá.

ICK!

"No time for kisses,"
Sophia told Noodle.
"We have a snoring solution to design."

Noodle twitched his ossicones.
"You're right," said Sophia.
"Step one is research.
Let's consult an expert."

ZZZZRRRRRR-WAHWWOOOO

ZZZZRRRRRRR-WAHWWOOOOOOOOOMP

"It's like a tuba being played by a jet engine,"
Sophia told Ms. Canticle, an acoustical engineer.

"Noodle's neck-to-lung-capacity ratio creates
a giant echo chamber," Ms. Canticle replied.
"If he had a shorter neck, he wouldn't snore
so loudly."

"If he had a shorter neck,
he wouldn't be a giraffe,"
said Sophia.

"Maybe if it were shaped differently," said Ms. Canticle.

That night Noodle hooked, crooked, and pretzeled his neck. But the problem persisted.

Father complained bitterly as he guzzled his coffee.

"Noodle's benefit to this family
is far outweighed by his costs,
which are fixed and perpetual."

"Perpetual?" asked Sophia.
"What's that mean?"

"Permanent," said Father. "Forever."

"Send him back,"
said Grand-mamá.

Noodle sadly sidled up
to Grand-mamá.

 Fluzzle,

  nuzzle,

SLUuuuuRP

YUCK!

"We need a better solution,"
Sophia told Ms. Canticle.

"Well…
if you can't
silence a sound,"
replied Ms. Canticle,
"you can block it or
transform it."

Block it?
Sophia and Noodle conferred.

"We'll need to build some prototypes," Sophia said.

That night, she handed Father some cotton wadding,
Mother earmuffs, Uncle Conrad earplugs,
and Grand-mamá a set of high-decibel
low-wavelength wireless sound-dampening
headphones she'd assembled
from spare parts.

Unfortunately,

ZZZZRRRRRR–WAHWW

OOOOOOOOOMP

ZZZZRRRRRR-WAHWWOOOOOOOOOMP

only Noodle slept.

"We had a family vote," groaned Uncle Conrad at breakfast. "My constituents demand an abiding solution."

"Abide— oh, permanent," said Sophia.

"Send him back."
Grand-mamá yawned.

Noodle eyed Grand-mamá.
His eyelashes fluzzled,
his nose—

"You'd better muzzle that nuzzle, mister," Grand-mamá warned.

Poor Noodle. His ossicones wilted.

"Chin up!" said Sophia. "We just need
to try a fresh approach."

She went to her room to design.

Six hours later,
she taped a detailed blueprint
to her workshop wall:

Sophia's Snore
Transformer

AIR
VENTS

ON

OFF

muzzle
Ir

"I need Father's briefcase,
Mother's gavel,
some crepe paper bunting,
two rolls of duct tape,
Grand-mamá's girdle,
and a spare flügelhorn
from Ms. Canticle,"
Sophia said.
She even cut a strip
from her favorite blue tutu.

That night,
when Noodle
donned his new
sleeping mask,

ZZZZRRRRRR-WAH
ZZZZRRRRRRR-V

WOOOOOOOOMP

HWWOOOOOOOOMP

became *hush-lala-hush hush-lala-hush*

like a sweet giraffian lullaby.

"Best sleep ever!"
declared Father,
pushing aside his coffee.

"I'm ready to seize the day!"
cried Mother,
dumping out her tea.

"I'm ready to seize
some pork,"
said Uncle Conrad,
chomping his
bacon.

Noodle fluzzled,
then he nuzzled,
and then . . .

Even Grand-mamá
looked better rested
and renewed, despite
the way she crossed
her strict arms.

KERRR-SCHMATZ!

Grand-mamá planted
the sloppiest kiss ever
on his cheek.

"We couldn't live without you, Noodle," she said.
"After all, you *are* family."

"Perdurably."

"Perpetually."

"Abidingly."

"Forever."

Glossary

Perdurable: permanent, lasting forever
Perpetual: permanent, lasting forever
Abiding: permanent, lasting forever

It takes forever to say some of those words!

Ossicones: the horn-like objects on a giraffe's head
Acoustical engineer: a person whose job involves the study
and control of sound
Prototype: a model of something being built for the first time